FIFA WORLD CUP

GLOBAL CITIZENS: SPORTS

Published in the United States of America by Cherry Lake Publishing
Ann Arbor, Michigan
www.cherrylakepublishing.com

Content Adviser: Liv Williams, Editor, www.iLivExtreme.com
Reading Adviser: Marla Conn, MS, Ed., Literacy specialist, Read-Ability, Inc.

Photo Credits: ©Maxisport/Shutterstock, cover, 1; ©Baldeagle17/Dreamstime, 5; ©Everett Historical/
Shutterstock, 6; ©Marco Iacobucci EPP/Shutterstock, 7, 22; © Paparazzofamily/Dreamstime, 8, 19;
©A.RICARDO/ Shutterstock, 10, 13; ©PA Images/Alamy Stock Photo, 15; ©evgenii mitroshin/Shutterstock, 16;
©mooinblack / Shutterstock, 20; ©Leszek Wrona/Dreamstime, 21; ©YutRedCap/Shutterstock, 23; ©AGIF/
Shutterstock, 24; ©Anton Gvozdikov/Shutterstock, 27; ©Denis Davydoff/Shutterstock, 28

Library of Congress Cataloging-in-Publication Data

Names: Hellebuyck, Adam, author. | Deimel, Laura, author.
Title: FIFA World Cup / written by Adam Hellebuyck and Laura Deimel.
Other titles: Fâedâeration Internationale de Football Association World Cup
Description: Ann Arbor, Michigan : Cherry Lake Publishing, [2019] | Series: Global Citizens: Sports |
    Audience: Grades 4 to 6 | Includes webography. | Includes bibliographical references and index.
Identifiers: LCCN 2019004156 | ISBN 9781534147478 (hardcover) | ISBN 9781534150331 (paperback) |
    ISBN 9781534148901 (pdf) | ISBN 9781534151765 (hosted ebook)
Subjects: LCSH: World Cup (Soccer)—History—Juvenile literature. | World Cup (Soccer)—Juvenile literature. |
    Fâedâeration Internationale de Football Association—History. | Soccer—Tournaments—History—Juvenile literature.
Classification: LCC GV943.49 .H45 2019 | DDC 796.334/668—dc23
LC record available at https://lccn.loc.gov/2019004156

Cherry Lake Publishing would like to acknowledge the work of the Partnership for 21st Century Learning.
Please visit *www.p21.org* for more information.

Printed in the United States of America
Corporate Graphics

ABOUT THE AUTHORS

Laura Deimel is a fourth grade teacher and Adam Hellebuyck is a high school social studies
teacher at University Liggett School in Grosse Pointe Woods, Michigan. They have worked
together for the past 8 years and are thrilled they could combine two of their passions, reading
and sports, into this work.

TABLE OF CONTENTS

CHAPTER 1

History: World Cup: Past and Present

The sport of soccer—called futbol or football in Europe—has over 200 million active players today! Soccer is organized by a group called FIFA, which stands for the Fédération Internationale de Football Association in French. This group makes the rules for soccer around the world.

In the Beginning . . .

Early in its **existence**, soccer did not have a championship tournament of its own. From 1908 to 1930, the only championship-like event for soccer was played in the Olympic Games.

Over time, more people were interested in following different soccer teams. After the 1928 Olympic Games, Jules Rimet,

Michigan Stadium in Ann Arbor, Michigan, and AT&T Stadium in Arlington, Texas, are one of the few stadiums in the United States that can hold more than 93,000 people.

the president of FIFA, wanted to host a soccer tournament separate from the Olympic Games. The first tournament, called the World Cup, happened in Uruguay in 1930. Thirteen teams from Europe, North America, and South America competed in the first World Cup. Uruguay won the tournament by beating Argentina in front of 93,000 soccer fans.

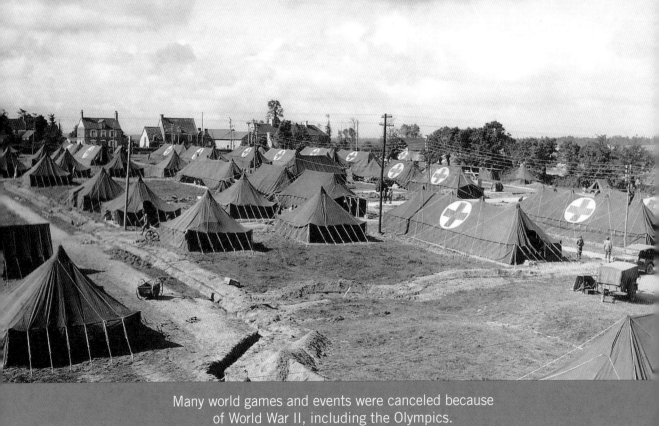

Many world games and events were canceled because
of World War II, including the Olympics.

A Tournament Every 4 Years

The first World Cup was so successful that FIFA decided to
hold another one. The tournament has happened every 4 years
since 1930, except for 1942 and 1946. World War II was happening
during those years, and some countries were fighting one another,
making a soccer competition impossible to hold.

During the FIFA World Cup, 32 teams from around the world compete in 64 matches over a 1-month period. That's a lot of matches!

The FIFA Women's World Cup trophy was originally designed in 1998.

Expanding the World Cup

In 1977, FIFA created a World Cup tournament for people under the age of 20. Today, this is called the FIFA U-20 World Cup, and it lets younger athletes play for their countries against other countries from around the world. The FIFA Women's World Cup was started in 1991 to allow female players to compete against teams from around the world.

[21ST CENTURY SKILLS LIBRARY]

The Trophy

The original trophy was called "Victory" but in 1946 was renamed the Jules Rimet Cup, after the man who helped create the World Cup tournament. During World War II, the Cup was hidden under the bed of an Italian sports official because people feared it would be stolen by the **Nazis**! While the Nazis never stole it, the Cup has been stolen multiple times from countries that won it.

Soccer vs. Football: What Is the Difference?

In the 1800s in England, football was played in a number of ways. There were three main styles. One was what Americans call soccer. Another became the sport called rugby. The third became the sport Americans call football. The word soccer was first used in England to explain a specific set of rules. Most people in England then referred to the game as soccer. During World War II, Americans in England learned the game and brought it back to the United States. In the 1980s, people in England stopped calling the game "soccer" because Americans were calling it that! They started calling the game "football."

The FIFA World Cup Trophy is made of real gold and weighs about 13.5 pounds (6 kilograms).

FIFA had a rule (now outdated) that allowed countries that won three championships to keep the trophy permanently. In 1970, Brazil became a three-time FIFA champion and was permanently awarded the trophy. However, in 1983 the trophy was stolen, and to this day, it has not been found!

In 1970, a new trophy was created and named the FIFA World Cup Trophy. That trophy isn't given to the champions—the original is kept under lock and key with FIFA. Winners are awarded a **replica**. FIFA plans on retiring the FIFA World Cup Trophy in 2038 and designing a new one in time for the 2042 World Cup.

Developing Questions

Think about when all the different World Cup tournaments began. The first World Cup for men began in 1930. The first World Cup for women began in 1991. The first World Cup for young athletes under 20 years old began in 1977. Why do you think these different World Cup tournaments were started in different years? What questions does this make you think of? Try to use the resources available to you here, in your library, and on the internet to help you find out.

CHAPTER 2

Geography: A Worldly Event

Countries hoping to host the FIFA World Cup tournament must make a "bid" to the FIFA Executive Committee. This committee is made up of soccer officials from different countries. In their bid, countries try to convince the Executive Committee that theirs is the best place to hold the World Cup. A country does this in a presentation. Countries talk about why soccer fans would want to visit their country and in what cities the tournament games could be held. Let's take a look at some of the countries that have hosted the World Cup.

The stadiums used during the World Cup are usually spread across the country hosting—sometimes almost 2,000 miles (3,218.6 kilometers) apart!

Uruguay

The first FIFA World Cup tournament was held in Uruguay, a country in South America, in 1930. Only 13 countries participated because it was difficult to travel long distances at that time. Most teams had to travel by ship or railroad. Now that people can travel more easily, more quickly, and more affordably in airplanes, more countries can participate in the World Cup. Uruguay won the World Cup again in 1950.

Uruguay's national soccer team has won 20 international titles in soccer, including the gold medal in the summer Olympic Games twice, 15 Copa América championships, and the 1980 Mundialito. The Mundialito was a tournament held in Uruguay between the previous winners of the World Cup. The Netherlands was also invited to attend because it had earned second place twice. The tournament was held in honor of the 50th anniversary of the first World Cup. In the final match of this tournament, Uruguay defeated Brazil by a score of 2–1. This was the same score when the two teams faced each other in the 1950 World Cup finals!

Hosting More Than Once

Five countries have hosted the FIFA World Cup more than once: Mexico, Italy, France, Germany, and Brazil. The World Cup will be held in the Middle East for the first time in 2022, in Qatar. In 2026, three countries will cohost the World Cup together for the first time: Canada, Mexico, and the United States.

There were a total of 97 goals scored during the 1974 World Cup.

Germany

When the World Cup was first created, FIFA decided that it would first be held in the Americas and then in Europe. The continents would then **alternate** hosting the tournament. The 1974 World Cup was held in West Germany, which at the time was separate from East Germany.

After World War II, Germany was **partitioned** into two different countries: West Germany and East Germany. These two countries

Brazil is the only country to have played in every World Cup tournament.

were **rivals**. In 1974, they competed against each other at the end of the first round of the World Cup. East Germany won that game, but West Germany went on to win the World Cup. Germany reunited as one country in 1990 and hosted the World Cup for the second time in 2006.

South Korea and Japan

Europe and the Americas alternated hosting the World Cup until 2002, when two countries in Asia (Japan and South Korea) were chosen to cohost the tournament. This was the first time that a tournament's matches would be held in two countries. When FIFA was first thinking about where to host the 2002 World Cup, Japan and South Korea were rivals. When the bidding was about to start, the two countries decided to come together and offer to hold the tournament in both their countries. As a result, FIFA **unanimously** chose them to cohost the tournament.

Gathering and Evaluating Sources

Imagine you are a member of the FIFA Executive Committee who has to decide where to hold the FIFA World Cup in 8 years. What information would you use to make your decision? Where would you find that information? What location would you select and why? Use information in your library and on the internet to help you make your decision.

Civics: Bringing People Together

Soccer is a global sport that has an effect on millions of people's lives. Even though countries compete against each other for the championship, the World Cup tournament is designed to bring people together—through the rules it creates and the programs it supports.

Ties in the Tournament

The FIFA World Cup **publicizes** many rules so the games can be fair and so fans and players can be well informed about the tournament. While regular-season soccer games can end in a tie, most of the World Cup games cannot. When a tie occurs,

The players' uniforms are usually designed using colors from the country's flag.
But some countries use colors that have a historical or political meaning.

The "Preliminary Competition" happens 3 years before every World Cup. Teams compete in matches in order to qualify for the 31 open spots.

the two teams play 30 minutes of extra time. If the teams are still tied at the end of those 30 minutes, they go to a penalty shootout, where each team takes turns kicking the ball from the penalty mark in front of the goal. Each team is given the same number of kicks on the goal. If one team is able to score and the other is not, that team is declared the winner. This ensures that each team is given a fair chance to win the game.

There were about 750 million people who watched the
FIFA Women's World Cup held in Canada in 2015.

During the 2018 FIFA World Cup in Russia, there were a total of 169 goals scored, or about 2.6 goals per match.

There were 219 yellow cards and 4 red cards given to players during the 2018 World Cup.

Yellow and Red Cards

A soccer official can give a penalty to a player who is unsportsmanlike, delays the game, celebrates too much, or argues with the official or other players. An official will usually give a player a yellow card for one of these actions. A yellow card is a warning that a player did something against the rules and should not do it again.

An official gives a player a red card for serious offenses, like attacking another player or **intentionally** breaking a rule to keep a goal from being scored. A player who receives a red card

The FIFA Diversity Award honors groups or programs that use soccer to build connections between people of different languages, races, religions, or cultures.

is ejected from the game. If this happens, that player's team has to play the rest of the game without a replacement. That means a team will only have 10 players against an opponent with 11 players.

These rules are designed to keep players safe by keeping the games fair and punishing bad behavior. Officials try their best to apply these rules to every game in the FIFA World Cup so all teams have a fair chance to win and athletes don't get hurt.

Helping Others

FIFA's mission is to keep improving the game of soccer and to get more people to play it. FIFA believes that people who work together to play soccer can work together in other ways to improve the world. FIFA uses some of the money raised by the World Cup tournament to support and help people around the world.

Soccer Without Borders is one of the many programs that benefits from the money raised. It was created in 2006. The program uses soccer to help young **refugees**. The organization helps these refugees learn teamwork and meet people in their new homelands. Soccer Without Borders earned FIFA's Diversity Award in 2017.

Developing Claims and Using Evidence

FIFA's mission is to use soccer to create a better world. What other specific examples can you find that show how the FIFA World Cup has helped make our world better? Research this topic further. Use the evidence you find to support your claim.

Economics: An Expensive Event

There is a lot of money involved in making sure the FIFA World Cup is a success. A soccer tournament with many different teams and hundreds of thousands of fans is expensive. It also has a big impact on the economy of the world as a whole.

Costs of the World Cup

The World Cup costs a lot of money to run. Soccer stadiums need to be built to hold large numbers of people (about 80,000 people per game). All the teams and fans need places to stay and eat while visiting the host cities, so sometimes new hotels, restaurants, and other places need to be built. In 2018, Russia hosted the World Cup at a cost of $11.6 billion. Much of this money was spent on building new stadiums. For example, the

According to reports, about 3.5 billion people worldwide watched the 2018 World Cup.

new Kaliningrad Stadium cost over $300 million to build. Russia also upgraded some of the existing stadiums. The Ekaterinburg Arena, which holds 35,000 people, cost $215 million to upgrade.

Making Money with the World Cup

While hosting the World Cup can be costly, it can also make FIFA and the host country a lot of money. In 2018, Russia reported that it would make $31 billion by the end of the tournament.

Because so many people watch the World Cup, businesses will **sponsor** the games in order to advertise their products.

FIFA is estimated to have made about $6 billion during the 2018 World Cup.

Some of the money that FIFA makes from the World Cup is given to charities, like Soccer Without Borders. Some is spent to hire

Taking Informed Action

The prize money for the winning team in the 2018 men's World Cup was $38 million. The prize money for the winning team in the 2019 Women's World Cup is predicted to be $4 million. Why do you think there is a huge gap between how much the men and women win? Write a letter to the president of FIFA explaining what you think, along with evidence to support your answer! You can find FIFA's mailing address on the official website.

people to work at the tournament and for FIFA in general. Some money is also spent to **promote** the game and the tournament around the world.

Prize Money for Winning Teams

The teams that play also receive money for winning games— and winning the whole tournament can earn a team a lot of money. At the men's World Cup in 2018, the winning team from France received $38 million. For FIFA's Women's World Cup in 2015, the winning team from the United States received $2 million. Some people have questioned why the men and women receive different amounts of prize money. FIFA is thinking about increasing the amount of money awarded to the women's winning team for future World Cups.

Communicating Conclusions

Did you know there are many different organizations involved with the FIFA World Cup that are trying to make the world a better place to live? Using your local library and the internet, find more organizations that work with FIFA and the World Cup to improve the lives of people around the world. Share what you learned with your friends and family.

Think About It

The costs of hosting the FIFA World Cup have changed from year to year. In 1990, Italy spent $4 billion to host the event. In 1994, the United States spent $500 million on the tournament. In 2018, Russia spent $11.6 billion on the World Cup. Using your understanding of math and research from your library or the internet, think about why the costs of the World Cup could change so much from year to year. What did each country need to spend money on in order to host the World Cup? Did each host country have a different number of fans attending? Would this make a difference in how much the country had to spend?

For More Information

Further Reading

FIFA World Football Museum. *The Official History of the FIFA World Cup*. London: Carlton Books, 2017.

Pettman, Kevin. *2018 FIFA World Cup Russia Fact File*. London: Carlton Kids, 2018.

Websites

FIFA World Football Museum
http://www.fifamuseum.com
This site shares the history of FIFA, the World Cup, and soccer around the world.

Grassroots FIFA—For Kids
https://grassroots.fifa.com/en/for-kids.html
Find information about how to play soccer, including techniques and the rules for playing the game.

GLOSSARY

alternate (AWL-tur-nate) take turns one after the other

existence (ig-ZIS-tuhns) something that is real, not imaginary

intentionally (in-TEN-shuh-nuhl-ee) doing something on purpose, not by accident

Nazis (NAHT-seez) members of the political group that ruled Germany from 1933 to 1945. Led by Adolf Hitler, the Nazis killed millions of Jews, Gypsies, and others before and during World War II

partitioned (pahr-TISH-uhnd) divided

promote (pruh-MOTE) to encourage something to happen

publicizes (PUHB-lih-size-iz) to make something well known

refugees (ref-yoo-JEEZ) people who have to flee from their homelands because they are in danger

replica (REP-lih-kuh) a copy exact in all details

rivals (RYE-vuhlz) people or countries who compete against each other often to be the best at something

sponsor (SPAHN-sur) to give a group or person money in exchange for something else, such as advertising

unanimously (yoo-NAN-uh-muhs-lee) to all agree

INDEX